Slinky Malinki

Lynley Dodd

Gareth Stevens Publishing
A WORLD ALMANAC EDUCATION GROUP COMPANY

Slinky Malinki
was blacker than black,
a stalking and lurking
adventurous cat.
He had bright yellow eyes,
a warbling wail
and a kink at the end
of his very long tail.

He was cheeky and cheerful,
friendly and fun,
he'd chase after leaves
and he'd roll in the sun.

But at night he was wicked
and fiendish and sly.
Through moonlight and shadow
he'd prowl and he'd pry.

He crept along fences,
he leaped over walls,
he poked into corners
and sneaked into halls.
What was he up to?
At night, to be brief,
Slinky Malinki
turned into a
THIEF.

All over town,
from basket and bowl,
he pilfered and pillaged,
he snitched and he stole.
Slippers and sausages,
biscuits, balloons,
brushes and bandages,
pencils and spoons.

He pulled them,
he dragged them,
he HEAVED them until . . .
he'd carried them home
to his house on the hill.

One rascally night
between midnight and four,
Slinky Malinki
stole MORE than before.
Some pegs and a teddy bear
dressed up in lace,
a gardening glove
from Macafferty's place.

A tatty old sneaker,
a smelly old sock
and Jennifer Turkington's
pottery smock.

A squishy banana,
some glue and a pen,
a cushion from
Oliver Tulliver's den.

A clock and some bottles,
a pair of blue jeans,
a half-knitted jersey,
a packet of beans.
He pulled them,
he dragged them,
he HEAVED them until . . .
he'd carried them home
to his house on the hill.

Then Slinky Malinki,
rapscallion cat,
piled them up high
in a heap on the mat.

The glue toppled over
and gummed up the pegs,
the jersey unraveled
and tangled his legs.
He tripped on the bottles
and slipped on the sock,
he tipped over sideways
and set off the clock.

CRASH went the bottles,
BEE-BEEP went the clock,
RO-RO-RO-RO
went the dogs on the block.
On went the lights,
BANG went the door
and out came the family,
one, two, three, four.

"Oh NO!" they all said,
"What a criminal cat!
Tomorrow we'll have to take
EVERYTHING back."
With a tangled-up middle
and glue on his face,
Slinky Malinki
was deep in disgrace.

NEVER again
did he answer the call,
when moon shadows danced
over garden and wall.
When whispers of wickedness
stirred in his head,
he adjusted his whiskers
and stayed home
instead.

Please visit our web site at: **www.garethstevens.com**
For a free color catalog describing Gareth Stevens' list of high-quality books and multimedia programs, call 1-800-542-2595 (USA) or 1-800-461-9120 (Canada). Gareth Stevens Publishing's Fax: (414) 332-3567.

Other GOLD STAR FIRST READER
Millennium Editions:

A Dragon in a Wagon
Find Me a Tiger
Hairy Maclary from Donaldson's Dairy
Hairy Maclary Scattercat
Hairy Maclary, Sit
Hairy Maclary and Zachary Quack
Hairy Maclary's Bone
Hairy Maclary's Caterwaul Caper
Hairy Maclary's Rumpus at the Vet
Schnitzel von Krumm's Basketwork
Slinky Malinki, Open the Door
The Smallest Turtle
SNIFF-SNUFF-SNAP!
Wake Up, Bear

and also by Lynley Dodd:

Hairy Maclary's Showbusiness
The Minister's Cat ABC
Schnitzel von Krumm Forget-Me-Not
Slinky Malinki Catflaps

Library of Congress Cataloging-in-Publication Data

Dodd, Lynley.
    Slinky Malinki / by Lynley Dodd.
        p. cm. — (Gold star first readers)
        Summary: The adventures of a mischievous black cat who turns into
    a thief at night.
        ISBN 0-8368-2784-8 (lib. bdg.)
        [1. Cats—Fiction. 2. Stories in rhyme.] I. Title. II. Series.
    PZ8.3.D637Sl 2001
    [E]—dc21   00-063549

This edition first published in 2001 by
Gareth Stevens Publishing
A World Almanac Education Group Company
330 West Olive Street, Suite 100
Milwaukee, WI 53212 USA

First published in New Zealand by Mallinson Rendel Publishers Ltd. Original © 1990 by Lynley Dodd.

Printed in Mexico

1 2 3 4 5 6 7 8 9 05 04 03 02 01